A Note to Parents and Teachers

Dorling Kindersley Classic Readers is a compelling new programme for beginning readers, designed in conjunction with leading literacy experts, including Cliff Moon M.Ed., Honorary Fellow of the University of Reading.

Beautiful illustrations and superb full-colour photographs combine with engaging, easy-to-read stories to offer a fresh approach to each subject in the series. Each *Dorling Kindersley Classic Reader* is guaranteed to capture a child's interest while developing his or her reading skills, general knowledge and love of reading.

The four levels of *Dorling Kindersley Classic Readers* are aimed at different reading abilities, enabling you to choose the books that are exactly right for your children.

Level One – Beginning to read
Level Two – Beginning to read alone
Level Three – Reading alone
Level Four – Proficient readers

The "normal" age at which a child begins to read can be anywhere from three to eight years old, so these levels are intended only as a general guideline.

No matter which level you select, you can be sure that you are helping your child learn to read, then read to learn!

www.dk.com

Created by Leapfrog Press Ltd

Project Editor Naia Bray-Moffatt
Art Editor Miranda Kennedy

For Dorling Kindersley
Senior Editor Marie Greenwood
Managing Art Editor Jacquie Gulliver
Managing Editor Joanna Devereux
Production Chris Avgherinos
Picture Researcher Liz Moore
Cover design Margherita Gianni

Reading Consultant
Cliff Moon M.Ed.

Published in Great Britain by
Dorling Kindersley Limited
9 Henrietta Street
London WC2E 8PS

2 4 6 8 10 9 7 5 3 1

Dorling Kindersley Classic Readers™ is a trademark
of Dorling Kindersley Limited, London.

A CIP catalogue record for this book is available from the
British Library.

ISBN 0-7513-6735-4

The publisher would like to thank the following for their
kind permission to reproduce their photographs:
Key b = below
AKG London: 27, 33b; Bridgeman Art Library: 45; Bruce
Coleman Collection: 6; Science & Society Picture Library: 37

Color reproduction by Colourscan, Singapore
Printed and bound in Belgium by Proost

Contents

Up the mountain   4

Aunt Detie visits   12

Mr Sesemann   22

Home again   28

Clara comes to stay   34

Glossary   48

DK CLASSIC READERS

READING **3** ALONE

HEIDI

A TIMELESS STORY OF CHILDHOOD

By Johanna Spyri

Adapted by Lucy Coats   Illustrated by Pamela Venus

DK

www.dk.com

London • New York • Sydney • Auckland • Delhi

Up the mountain

One June morning, Heidi trudged up
the mountain behind her Aunt Detie.
Heidi's parents were dead and Detie
couldn't look after her any longer.

Detie was taking Heidi to live with her grandfather.

They climbed high up the mountain to a wooden hut in some fir trees, where an old man was sitting on a rough bench.

Heidi ran up to him. "Hello, Grandfather!" she said. The old man stared at her.

"Here is the child, Uncle," said Detie. "She must stay with you now."

"Ho!" said Grandfather, frowning. "She must, must she? Well leave her here and go away then!"

Wooden home

Heidi has gone to live in the mountains in Switzerland called the Alps. Mountain huts, like Grandfather's, were made of strong wood to keep out the wind and the cold.

Heidi began to explore her new home. She peeped into the goat stall, ran around the three fir trees and then went indoors with Grandfather.

"Where shall I sleep?" she asked.

"Wherever you like, child," replied Grandfather.

Heidi wanted to sleep in the loft. Soon she and Grandfather had made a cosy bed out of soft hay.

"It's just perfect!" Heidi exclaimed.

"Time to eat now," said Grandfather. He put some toasted bread and cheese in front of her and Heidi ate hungrily. She couldn't believe how good everything tasted.

As dusk fell, a boy called Peter appeared with Grandfather's goats. Heidi said goodnight to her new friends and skipped happily up to bed.

Early next morning, Heidi and Peter
took the goats to the grassy pasture.
Heidi ran around the meadow picking
flowers. Peter taught her the names of
all the goats. Her special favourite was
a little white goat called Snowflake.

On the way home, Heidi cried out in
amazement. The mountains
seemed to be on fire!

But Grandfather
told her it was
only the sun
saying goodnight.

Grandfather told Heidi
more stories of the
mountains while
she ate her
supper.

Winter soon came
and one day it snowed heavily.
Grandfather wrapped Heidi up warmly
and they sledged down the side of the
mountain to visit Peter's Granny.

"Here I am, Granny!" called Heidi.
The old lady held out her hands.

"Come to me, my child, for I can't
see you."

"Let me open the shutters, Granny. Then you will see me." The old woman shook her head sadly and told Heidi that she was blind. Heidi was sorry for her and promised to come and see her every day.

So all winter long Heidi kept Granny company, while Grandfather mended her rickety old hut.

Aunt Detie visits

In the early spring,
Aunt Detie visited Heidi
and Grandfather again.
She said that she was taking
Heidi to Frankfurt to be a
companion to a little girl
who was in a wheelchair.
The girl had no mother
and her father was often
away, so she
was lonely.

Train journey

Trains were the quickest kind of transport in those days. It still took Heidi about two days to travel across Europe from the Swiss Alps to her new home in Frankfurt.

Grandfather was furious with Detie.

"Heidi's healthy and happy where she is," he said.

"I won't come! I won't!" yelled poor Heidi. "I want to stay here with Grandfather." But it was no use.

A determined Aunt Detie packed Heidi's clothes and dragged the crying girl down the mountain and aboard the train. Heidi did not even have time to say goodbye to anyone.

In the house in Frankfurt, Clara Sesemann sat with Miss Rottenmeier the housekeeper, waiting for her new friend. Soon there was a knock at the door and Heidi and Aunt Detie arrived. Miss Rottenmeier was rather unhappy about Heidi's shabby clothes.

"She really will not do at all!" she said.

Heidi and Clara soon made friends, but Heidi was still homesick. Everything here was strange, even suppertime.

This was not like Grandfather's hut at all. Miss Rottenmeier gave her a long lecture on how to behave but Heidi was so tired that she fell asleep in the middle of it.

Lesson-time next morning was worse. Heidi heard a rustling like the wind through the fir trees at home. She ran to the window, knocking over an inkwell in her hurry to see the trees, but it was only some carriages passing. Clara laughed, but Miss Rottenmeier was furious with Heidi.

While Clara rested after lunch, Heidi went out to explore. She soon found a church with a high tower and begged the caretaker to let her climb to the top. But all she could see were chimneys and roofs instead of her beloved mountains.

Seeing how sad Heidi looked, the caretaker gave her some kittens.

"Take two now and I'll deliver the rest," he said. Heidi was delighted and skipped home with them in her pocket.

Next morning a big basket appeared for Heidi at lesson-time. Clara wanted to know what was inside, and she didn't have to wait long.

The lid was not fastened properly, and suddenly there were kittens everywhere.

"Oh look! How pretty," exclaimed Clara, as one climbed onto her knee. But some of them tried to claw their way up Miss Rottenmeier's skirt.

She screamed and danced
about the floor in terror.

"Oh! Oh! Oh! Get rid
of these horrid creatures!"
She turned to Heidi. "You dreadful
child! You shall be shut up in
the cellar with the rats as
your punishment!"

But Clara said,
"Oh, please wait until
Papa comes home.
I promise to tell
him everything.
Let him decide
what should
happen to Heidi."

Reluctantly,
Miss Rottenmeier
agreed.

For a few days afterwards, nothing else went wrong. But this did not stop Heidi from feeling homesick. She missed Grandfather and Granny and the sun saying goodnight to the mountains. She decided to run away. She packed up all her belongings and was about to set off when she met Miss Rottenmeier.

"Where do you think you're going?" demanded Miss Rottenmeier.

"Home," said Heidi bravely.

"You ungrateful child!" scolded Miss Rottenmeier, as she snatched her bundle away. "Look at these things! They're a disgrace and I shall throw them in the rubbish bin."

Heidi cried and cried at the loss of her precious belongings and even Clara and the kittens could not comfort her.

Mr Sesemann

A few days later Clara's father arrived home from his travels abroad.

Miss Rottenmeier soon had a word with him.

"Heidi's behaviour is terrible and she brings dreadful animals into the house. I think she is mad!"

"She seems normal enough to me," said Mr Sesemann. "But I shall ask Clara what she thinks."

Clara told him about the inkwell and the kittens. Her father laughed.

"So you don't want Heidi to go home then?"

"Oh no, Papa!"

Mr Sesemann went back to see Miss Rottenmeier.

"Heidi will stay," he said firmly. "Clara loves having her here. And I shall ask my mother to look after Heidi when she arrives next week."

The next week, Grandmamma Sesemann arrived. She sat down with Heidi and put her arm around her.

"What have you learnt in your lessons, my dear?" she asked.

"Nothing," sighed Heidi. "Reading is too difficult!"

Grandmamma smiled. "If you work hard, I will give you this book!"

The book had beautiful pictures of meadows and mountains that reminded Heidi of home. Her eyes shone. "I wish I could read now!" she exclaimed.

One morning, about a week later, Grandmamma peeped into the study. There was Heidi reading to Clara!

"I can do it! I can read!" she cried.

That evening, Heidi found the beautiful book by her place at supper.

"It is yours for always," said Grandmamma.

Soon afterwards, strange things
began to happen in the
Sesemann house.
The servants said
that they had
heard noises and
seen a ghost!

Mr Sesemann decided to investigate with his friend, Dr Classen. Late one night they saw a little white figure in the moonlight.

"Who's there?" they shouted.

The figure turned round. It was Heidi.

"Have you been dreaming?" asked Dr Classen.

"Oh yes," said Heidi. "I dreamt I was with Grandfather. But then I woke up and I'm still here!" She began to cry.

Dr Classen talked to Mr Sesemann.

"Heidi is terribly homesick. You must send her back straight away!"

Sleepwalking

People who are unhappy may walk while they are sleeping. They can't remember sleepwalking when they wake up.

Home again

Heidi couldn't believe that she was going home at last. Clara promised Heidi that she would visit and they kissed goodbye.

The long train journey passed in a flash and soon Heidi was running into Peter's hut and hugging Granny.

Grandfather was sitting on the bench outside his hut, just as he had been when Heidi first saw him. Heidi ran to him crying, "Grandfather!" and threw her arms around him. Both their eyes were wet with tears.

"So you've come back then," he said. "Did they send you away?"

"Oh no," said Heidi. She tried to tell Grandfather what had happened, then gave him a letter from Mr Sesemann which explained everything.

There was a shrill whistle from the mountainside. It was Peter and the goats. He stared at Heidi, amazed.

"I'm so glad you're home," he said.

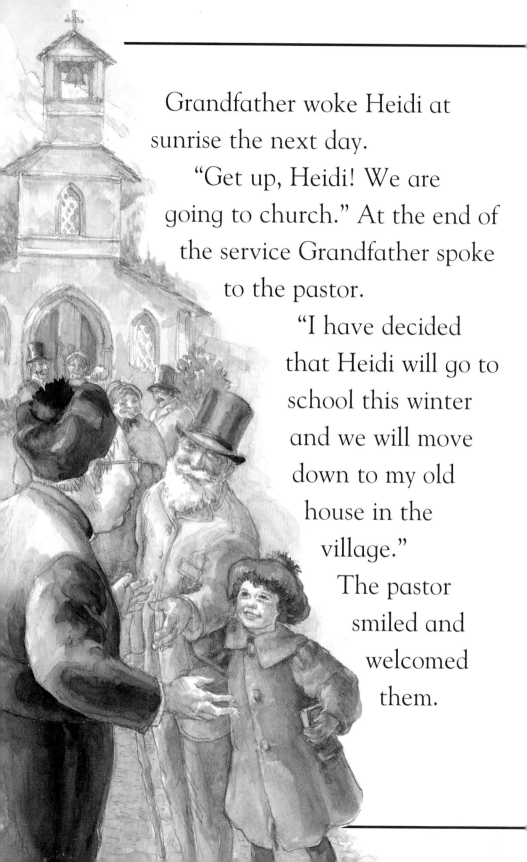

Grandfather woke Heidi at sunrise the next day.

"Get up, Heidi! We are going to church." At the end of the service Grandfather spoke to the pastor.

"I have decided that Heidi will go to school this winter and we will move down to my old house in the village."

The pastor smiled and welcomed them.

One morning Dr Classen arrived. He explained that Clara had been very ill and couldn't come to visit until the summer. He brought presents and food from her and soon Grandfather had prepared a wonderful picnic.

Dr Classen ate hungrily. "Clara will certainly get well when she comes here!" he exclaimed.

That winter, as promised, Grandfather and Heidi moved down to an old house in the village.

Every morning Heidi went to school and worked hard. But Peter always played truant. He didn't like lessons. Grandfather got very cross with him.

Granny was ill when Heidi next went to visit.

"Poor Granny," she said.

"I wish that I could read to you every day."

Then Heidi had a brilliant idea. She would teach Peter to read to Granny. Peter reluctantly agreed. Heidi began by teaching him his alphabet from a book Clara had given her. Then one day Peter astonished Granny by reading her a whole hymn. He was very proud.

Alphabet book

Heidi helps Peter learn his letters with a German alphabet book like this. Knowing his ABC helps Peter learn to read.

Clara comes to stay

One spring morning, when Heidi and Grandfather had moved back to the hut, Peter brought them a letter from Frankfurt. Heidi opened it.

"Clara is coming!" Heidi cried excitedly. "Hooray!"

But Peter was not so pleased. He was frightened that Heidi would go away and leave him again.

Six weeks later, Heidi saw a strange procession of people climbing the mountainside. "They've come!" she cried and ran to meet them.

Grandfather lifted Clara into her wheelchair.

Heidi pushed her all around the hut.

"How lovely it is," cried Clara, as Grandfather carried her up to show her Heidi's hayloft. "Can I sleep here, too?"

Grandmamma arranged to stay in the nearby village and agreed to come and visit soon. The two girls were overjoyed.

Clara felt stronger
as each day passed.
She began to try
to get out of her
wheelchair.

Wheelchair

Many people with disabilities could not afford wheelchairs. Clara is lucky that she can. She has a wheelchair that was made specially for her.

Soon she begged to go to the pasture with the goats. But Peter was jealous.

One morning, Peter saw Clara's empty wheelchair outside the hut. In a rage, he hurled it down the steep slope. Now Clara would have to go home, he thought to himself. Then he ran away without even waiting for the goats.

When Grandfather came around the corner carrying Clara he looked everywhere for the wheelchair. But it was nowhere to be found.

When they found the smashed wheelchair, Clara cried, because now she wouldn't be able to go to the pasture. Grandfather hated to see her so upset and decided to carry Clara all the way to the pasture himself.

When they arrived, Peter was already there, and Grandfather asked if he had seen Clara's chair. "No," said Peter, but Grandfather looked at him thoughtfully.

 Clara and Heidi spent a happy morning playing with the goats. After lunch, Heidi wanted to show Clara the lovely flowers in the meadow higher up. She asked Peter to help her lift Clara, and he felt so guilty that he agreed.

With Heidi and Peter's help, Clara
put one foot in front of the other.

"Look!" she exclaimed. "I can walk!"
Grandfather was delighted.

Clara practised her walking every
day until Grandmamma's next visit.
Grandmamma stared in amazement as
Clara walked slowly towards her.

"How can I ever thank you? It's a
miracle!" she gasped to Grandfather.

"Just God's sun and good mountain air!" Grandfather smiled back.

One afternoon, as Peter was going to the village, he met a stranger who asked him the way to Heidi's hut.

"A policeman, come to arrest me for smashing the chair," thought Peter, as he ran away, terrified.

"What an odd, shy boy," said Mr Sesemann to himself as he continued on his way up the mountain.

Clara's father laughed to himself as he got closer to Grandfather's hut. His business trip had finished early and he was looking forward to surprising Clara. "They'll have such a shock when they see me!" he chuckled. But it was

Mr Sesemann who had the shock instead.

As he came nearer the hut he stood and stared, and his eyes filled with tears.

"Don't you know me, Papa?" cried Clara, walking straight towards him.

"Is it possible?" he whispered, as he took her in his arms. Then Grandmamma joined them.

"You must meet Heidi's grandfather."

While Mr Sesemann thanked Grandfather from the bottom of his heart for helping Clara to walk, Grandmamma saw Peter sneaking by.

"Young man," she called. "Why are you looking so guilty?" Peter turned red, blushing with shame as he confessed about Clara's wheelchair.

"What you did was very wrong," said Grandmamma. "But since you are sorry for what you did, you are forgiven."

Grandmamma understood how jealous Peter had been of Clara's friendship with Heidi. Then she asked him what he would like as a present to remember them by. For the first time in his life, Peter could have anything he wanted. He thought and thought, then he asked for a penny. Grandmamma laughed and promised him a penny a week for life. Peter couldn't believe his luck and skipped away, overjoyed!

Later, Mr Sesemann asked Grandfather how he could reward him for all he had done for his daughter.

"It is reward enough to see Clara so well," said Grandfather. "But if you promise me that you will take care of Heidi when I die, that would make me very happy," said Grandfather, and the two men shook hands on it.

All too soon the time came for Clara, Mr Sesemann and Grandmamma to say goodbye, but Clara promised to visit them next summer.

One penny
Peter could buy as much with a penny as you can buy with £10 now. This is an English penny from the time Heidi's story was written.

That was not the end of the story. Shortly afterwards, Dr Classen retired and bought Grandfather's old ramshackle house in the village. He had it rebuilt so that Heidi and Grandfather could still live in one half in the winter. Grandfather became the doctor's best friend and taught him all the ways of the mountains.

"Heidi seems like my own daughter," he said to Grandfather one day. "May I help you take care of her?"

Grandfather shook his hand. "That would be wonderful," he smiled.

So Heidi spent another happy winter down in the village.

There she was
surrounded by
people who
loved and
cared for her.

Glossary

Alps
A range of high mountains in Europe. The Alps stretch across many countries, including Switzerland, France, Germany, Italy, Austria and what used to be Yugoslavia.

Carriage
A vehicle with wheels used for carrying people, usually drawn by horses. Carriages have now been replaced by cars.

Determined
A determined person has set his or her mind on something and will not change it.

Goatherd
A person who raises many goats for wool and for milk, which may be made into delicious cheese.

Guilty
A guilty person has done something wrong or feels that he or she has behaved badly.

Hay
Grass or another such plant that has been cut and dried for feeding animals. Hay may be stored in a hayloft.

Housekeeper
A person hired to manage someone else's home. A housekeeper often lives in the home they manage.

Hymn
A song praising God. Hymns are often sung during religious ceremonies such as church services.

Inkwell
A pot that holds ink. Inkpens are dipped in an inkwell and filled with ink before writing.

Pastor
A member of the clergy who is in charge of a church. A pastor may also be called a priest or a minister.

Pasture
The grassy land where sheep and cattle can graze.

Sleepwalking
When a person gets up and walks or even talks while they are sleeping.

Truant
Children who play truant do not go to school when they should.